Disney
Winnie the Pooh

It's Fun to Learn

A Surprise Garden

It was early summer in the Hundred-Acre Wood. Rabbit's garden was filled with flowers and vegetables that were ready for picking.

"How does your garden grow?" Pooh asked Rabbit.

"Those vegetables stay hidden underneath the dirt," Tigger said. "Then Ol' Long Ears digs up the loot when it's ready—just like buried treasure."

"Not exactly," said Rabbit. "First I plant these itty bitty things called seeds."
Rabbit held out a hand to show his friends what they looked like.

"And, as a little surprise, I have a packet for each of you. These are my special 'surprise' seeds. You'll have to plant them and see what grows."

"Oh, my!" said Piglet. "I don't know much about planting a garden."

"Nonsense," said Owl. "Like my old Uncle Cuthbert used to say, 'Just give them some room and the flowers will bloom!'"

"Flowers and vegetables do need room to grow," said Rabbit. "There are some simple rules to planting. If you follow them, your seeds will sprout."

"Hoo-hoo-hoo!" shouted Tigger. "Sproutin', shoutin' seeds—I can hardly wait!"

"Now, listen carefully," said Rabbit, "and I'll tell you my rules:

    Till and hoe; pull out the weeds.

    Then dig a hole to hold the seeds.

    Plant them in a sunny spot.

    Then water them, but not a lot.

    There's one more thing you need to know...

    It takes some time for seeds to grow."

Next, Rabbit gave each of his friends a little patch of dirt in his garden where they could plant their seeds.

"A honey tree would be the perfect plant for me," Pooh said.

"I betcha I'll grow a stupenderous beanstalk up to the sky!" cried Tigger. "C'mon, Long Ears! Let's get a-plantin'!"

Pooh and his friends followed Rabbit's directions carefully.
First, Pooh and Piglet hoed and raked the soil. Next, Tigger dug
some perfect-sized holes. Finally, Roo planted the seeds in a sunny spot,
while Owl carefully watered them.

Now came the hard part—waiting for the seeds to grow.

Each day, Pooh and his friends stopped by Rabbit's garden to check on their seeds. And each day they went away feeling a little disappointed because they didn't see anything growing.

"These seeds have got lots of catchin' uppin' to do!" Tigger said with a sigh.

Poor Roo couldn't wait much longer. "What if the seeds don't sprout, and we run out of patience?" he asked.

"Now, now," said Rabbit. "You've got to give the seeds a chance! Everything grows in its own time. Take good care of your seeds, give them sunlight and water, and I promise they'll grow."

Pooh looked very thoughtful. "Perhaps we didn't follow Rabbit's gardening rules," he said.

"Fiddlesticks!" said Owl, shaking his head. "We did exactly what he told us to do."

Suddenly Roo had an idea. "Sometimes Mama takes extra special care of me with a little treat," he said.

"Hey, I think you got something there, Roo Boy!" said Tigger. "We each need to do something extra special for our seeds."

So each of Pooh's friends came up with his very own "seed-caring" idea. Piglet covered his patch of dirt with a soft, pink blanket, so his seeds wouldn't get cold.

Tigger put on his good luck hat and did his tiggerific rain dance.
"Hoo-hoo-hoo!" he cried. "Rain, rain, shower, shower! Bring down some flower power!"

Owl tickled his patch of dirt with a feather to cheer up his seeds. "Won't they be tickled pink!" he said.

Meanwhile, Roo and Piglet hurried over to Roo's house to get his magic wand. When Roo returned to the garden, he waved it over his little patch. Then he did the same thing for each of his friends' seed patches.

"Abracadabra, alakazoo!" cried Roo. "Please grow for Tigger, Owl, Piglet, and Pooh!"

Shortly thereafter, Pooh went home to get his honey pot. When he came back to the garden, he sprinkled the dirt with tiny drops of honey.

"Bother," said Pooh. "I do hope this sweetens them up. Honey always works for me!"

A few days later, all the seeds began to sprout.

First, Pooh's friends saw little buds on the flower stems and baby vegetables. Then the buds turned into blooms and the vegetables got bigger.

"What a spectaculous surprise these seeds turned out to be!" cried Tigger.

There were bright yellow sunflowers for Tigger, pink pansies for Piglet, string beans for Owl, cherry tomatoes for Roo, … but nothing for Pooh.

Poor Pooh looked up at Tigger's tall, sunny flowers. He couldn't figure out why his seeds weren't growing.

"Think, think, think," he said. "I think I did everything I was supposed to do. I've even tried to be patient."

Pooh's friends were so pleased with their little crop of vegetables and flowers that they decided to pick some for Rabbit as a thank-you present.

First, Tigger cut down his sunflowers. And when he did, the garden area was suddenly bathed in sunlight.

"Ol' Long Ears will absotively love my blossomin' bloomers!" said Tigger.

A few days later, the most surprising thing happened. With Tigger's flowers out of the way, the sun began to shine right on Pooh's garden patch. And his seeds began to sprout and grow. Pooh's seeds grew into the best plant of all!

"Those are the biggest, plumpest strawberries I've ever seen!" said Rabbit.

"Oh, thank you," said Pooh, although he wasn't sure what he had done.

"It just goes to show: patience works wonders, Pooh," said Rabbit.

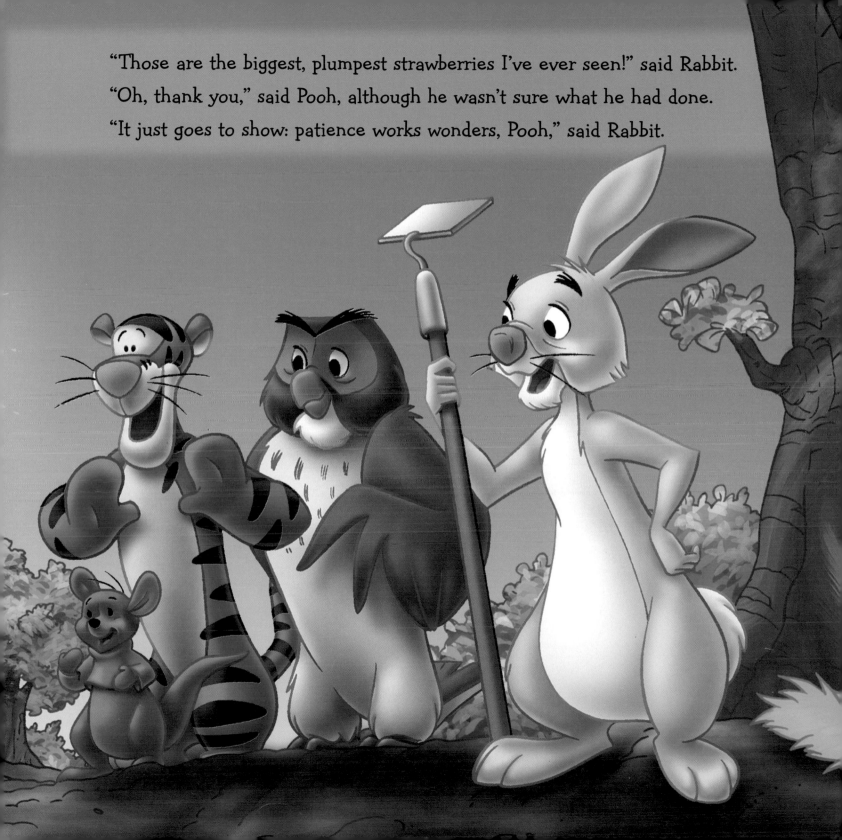

"I'll have to add 'patience' to my list of gardening rules," said Rabbit.

Make sure you find a sunny spot

Then till and rake and hoe.

Be patient! It may take awhile...

To see your garden grow!

Fun to Learn Activity

Yes, indeedy. A garden is hard work, but your plants will grow if you follow the rules. See if you can go back and find all the different kinds of flowers, fruits, and vegetables my friends grew from their surprise seeds!

With a little help from your parents, try your hand at planting or watering the flowers in your own backyard! Be sure to follow Rabbit's gardening rules.